Fixing Fences

by Bruce Wannamaker
illustrated by
Jenny Williams

Published by The Dandelion House
A Division of The Child's World

for distribution by VICTOR

BOOKS a division of SP Publications, Inc.

WHEATON, ILLINOIS 60187

Offices also in
Whitby, Ontario, Canada
Amersham-on-the-Hill, Bucks, England

Published by The Dandelion House, A Division of The Child's World, Inc.

A Book for Competent Readers.

Library of Congress Cataloging in Publication Data

————————————— .

Fixing fences.

Summary: Laura has to work hard at forgiving her
neighbors whom she feels are responsible for the loss
of her pet goat.
[1. Forgiveness—Fiction.   2. Christian life—Fic-
tion]   I. Williams, Jenny, 1939-   ill.   II. Title.
PZ7.M739Fi   1984   [E]   84-7037
ISBN 0-89693-226-5

1 2 3 4 5 6 7 8 9 10 11 12 R 90 89 88 87 86 85 84

Fixing Fences

"If you hold anything against
anyone, forgive him. . . ."
—Mark 11:25 (NIV)

It all started because Uncle Ned's goat had three
little kids. The mother goat could feed only two of
them, so Uncle Ned brought one kid, wrapped in
an old sweater, to Laura.

"Maa," cried the little kid.

Laura laughed. "I'm not your mama," she said,
"but I'll take good care of you." She held the tiny
bundle in her arms. "I'll name you Gretchen."

As Uncle Ned left, he said, "I'll come and get her when she is big enough to take care of herself."

Laura's mom agreed. "Our yard isn't big enough for a full-grown goat."

"And our neighbors might object to a farm animal anyway," said Dad.

"But we have a fence around the yard," said Laura.

"That reminds me," said Dad. "The side fence needs fixing. I must take care of that."

But first, Dad made a little house for Gretchen. Laura filled it with fresh hay. Within a few days, Gretchen followed Laura around the yard and drank milk from a bottle.

After a week or so, Gretchen could nibble grass
and honeysuckle. And it did not take her long to
discover the broken fence rail.

One morning she jumped right through the fence
and into the Underwoods' vegetable garden.

She nibbled some lettuce and carrot tops and was
feasting on string beans when Mrs. Underwood
screamed, "Get out of there!"

Gretchen kept right on eating until the Underwoods' dog, Queenie, chased her back over the fence.

But Gretchen did not stay in her own yard for long. In no time she jumped the broken fence again. She ate the geraniums right out of the window box on the Underwoods' front porch.

This time both Mrs. Underwood and Queenie chased Gretchen back home.

"Laura," called Mrs. Underwood, "you simply must keep that goat off our property before she gets into our prize roses. Why don't you fix your fence?"

"We will. I promise," said Laura as she held Gretchen.

Later, Mom tied one of Laura's hair ribbons around Gretchen's neck.

"I must get a real collar for Gretchen," she said.

"And a better rope," said Laura as they tied Gretchen to a tree.

"She will have to stay tied until Dad can fix the fence," said Mom.

Dad was going to fix the fence on Saturday, but early Saturday morning he was called away on business.

"Laura, keep Gretchen tied," he said as he left the house.

So Laura kept Gretchen tied to the tree. But Gretchen didn't like it and kept walking around the tree until she was all tangled up.

Laura untied the rope. "How could you get into such a mess?" she asked.

Just then, her friend Amy came by on her bike.

"Guess what? Aunt Emily brought me a new computer game — want to see it?" Amy asked.

"Sure," said Laura. Very quickly she tied Gretchen to the tree again. "Be a good kid," she called as she rode off on her bike.

But Gretchen wanted to be free. She tugged and tugged on the rope. After awhile, the rope began to loosen.

One final tug and Gretchen was free! Over the fence she went for the third time. She headed straight for the Underwoods' prize roses.

She was eating blossoms, stems, and all when Mr. Underwood dashed out. He grabbed Gretchen, and, with Queenie barking at his heels, dragged Gretchen home.

"I'm going to call the sheriff," he shouted angrily.

"Oh, please don't!" cried Laura's mom. "I'm really sorry. Please forgive us for being so careless."

"Just get rid of that goat. She has ruined our roses!"

"Oh, no! I'm sorry! We've tried to keep Gretchen tied while waiting for my husband to fix the fence. I realize now we should have fixed it even if we had to hire someone to do it. We will get it fixed today."

"Just get rid of the goat. It's too late to talk about fences! I never want to see that goat again."

"Laura will be heartbroken!"

"Just get rid of that goat!"

"We'll send her back to the goat farm," promised Laura's mom.

"The sooner, the better," Mr. Underwood muttered as he left.

That very afternoon Uncle Ned came to get Gretchen. Laura was very upset.

"It's not fair," she sobbed. "The Underwoods are grouches! I don't like them any more."

"Now Laura," said Mom, "the Underwoods are our neighbors."

"I don't care," Laura sobbed. "It's their fault Gretchen has to go away so soon."

"You can come and see Gretchen anytime," said Uncle Ned. "She'll always be your goat."

"But she can't stay here with me—all because of the Underwoods!" Laura felt very angry and hurt inside.

The next morning was Sunday. Laura was still angry as she dressed for Sunday School. And when she got there, she didn't feel any better.

The lesson was about forgiveness.

"You know," said Miss Eaton, "Jesus said we should forgive others, not just once, but over and over again."

"Even when they do mean things?" asked Laura.

"God forgives us when we do mean things," said Miss Eaton. "And we should forgive others. Isn't that what the Bible says?"

"Sometimes I fight with my brother," said Amy. "Then when I tell him I'm sorry, he forgives me."

"When I broke my sister's pocket radio, I told her I was really sorry," said Peter, "and she forgave me."

"Well, I can't forgive the Underwoods," said Laura. "They made me send Gretchen back to Uncle Ned's farm."

"Laura," said Miss Eaton, "God can help you forgive. God can take away your anger and help you love the Underwoods. Shouldn't a Christian love and forgive?"

"I guess," said Laura. "But it's hard."

"Sure it's hard," said Miss Eaton. "But it's the right thing to do, isn't it?"

Laura nodded. Still, she felt angry.

That evening Laura sat with her mom on the porch. For awhile they just sat there quietly.

"You miss Gretchen, don't you?" said Mom.

Laura nodded.

"I know how you feel, but you couldn't have kept Gretchen forever anyway."

"But the Underwoods made me send her away too soon," said Laura.

Laura pointed her finger toward her neighbors' house. "They're mean," she said.

Mom listened quietly. Then she said, "Laura, I want to share a secret your grandfather shared with me a long time ago. Look carefully at my hand as I point my finger at the Underwoods' house. How many fingers are pointing back at me?"

Laura counted three.

"You see," said Mom. "It was mostly our fault that Gretchen could not stay here. It was partly Dad's fault for not fixing the fence. It was partly my

fault for not getting a better collar for Gretchen,
and partly your fault for not tying her up more
tightly on Saturday. Three fingers are pointing back
at us, right?''

"Oh, I guess you're right," said Laura.

Mom gave Laura a hug.

"You know what? We're the ones who need to be forgiven. We should have taken better care of Gretchen."

"Maybe," said Laura. "But I'm still angry about it."

"Well, Laura, the Bible says we should never keep anger in our hearts, but ask God to help us forgive."

"Why, that's what Miss Eaton told us," said Laura.

"Let's do it," said Mom. "Let's each say a silent prayer right here."

And they did.

As soon as Dad came home from his trip, he fixed the broken fence.

Later he said to Laura, "It's easier to fix fences than feelings. I've apologized to Paul Underwood, but I can't grow new prize roses for him in time for the rose show!

"I wish there was some little thing we could do to help make up for the hard feelings we've had these last few weeks."

Laura went into the kitchen. Mom was making a spice cake for the church picnic. Suddenly, Laura had an idea.

"Maybe I could make a spice cake for the Underwoods," she said. "Just to say we're sorry."

"That would be a very thoughtful thing to do," said Mom.

Laura went right to work. She mixed the butter
and sugar together, then added eggs, molasses,
flour, spices and milk. She baked the cake in the
oven, and while it was still warm, took it next door
to the Underwoods.

"Thanks, Laura," said Mrs. Underwood. "What a
lovely thing to do. And Laura . . . we *are* sorry
about Gretchen."

Then, a few weeks later, Mr. Underwood called Laura on the telephone. "Laura, I have a surprise for you. Come on over."

Laura ran next door. Mr. Underwood led her into the kitchen. There in a box by the stove was Queenie with four baby puppies.

"Oh," sighed Laura. "They are the cutest puppies I've ever seen."

"You can have the pick of the lot," said Mr. Underwood. "I've already asked your mom and dad."

Laura picked up the spotted one. "This one. I'll take this one, and I'll call him Prince."

"As soon as he is old enough, you can take him home," said Mrs. Underwood.

"And he can play in both yards," said Laura. "Because he has family on both sides of the fence."

"Right!" said Mr. Underwood with a smile.